"I DON'T LIKE CHOOSE YOUR OWN ADVENTURE® BOOKS. I *LOVE* THEM!" says Jessica Gordon, age ten. And now, kids between the ages of six and nine can choose their own adventures too. Here's what kids have to say about the Skylark Choose Your Own Adventure® books.

"These are my favorite books because you can pick whatever choice you want—and the story is all about you."
—**Katy Alson,** *age 8*

"I love finding out how my story will end."
—**Joss Williams,** *age 9*

"I like all the illustrations!"
—**Savitri Brightfield,** *age 7*

"A six-year-old friend and I have lots of fun making the decisions together."
—**Peggy Marcus** *(adult)*

Bantam Skylark Books in the Choose Your Own
     Adventure® Series
Ask your bookseller for the books you have missed

 #1 THE CIRCUS
 #2 THE HAUNTED HOUSE
 #3 SUNKEN TREASURE
 #4 YOUR VERY OWN ROBOT
 #5 GORGA, THE SPACE MONSTER
 #6 THE GREEN SLIME
 #7 HELP! YOU'RE SHRINKING
 #8 INDIAN TRAIL
 #9 DREAM TRIPS
#10 THE GENIE IN THE BOTTLE
#11 THE BIGFOOT MYSTERY
#12 THE CREATURE FROM MILLER'S POND
#13 JUNGLE SAFARI
#14 THE SEARCH FOR CHAMP
#15 THE THREE WISHES
#16 DRAGONS!
#17 WILD HORSE COUNTRY
#18 SUMMER CAMP
#19 THE TOWER OF LONDON
#20 TROUBLE IN SPACE
#21 MONA IS MISSING
#22 THE EVIL WIZARD
#23 THE POLAR BEAR EXPRESS
#24 THE MUMMY'S TOMB
#25 THE FLYING CARPET

THE FLYING CARPET

JIM RAZZI

ILLUSTRATED BY FRANK BOLLE

An Edward Packard Book

A BANTAM SKYLARK BOOK®
TORONTO · NEW YORK · LONDON · SYDNEY · AUCKLAND

RL 2, 007–009

THE FLYING CARPET

A Bantam Book / March 1985

CHOOSE YOUR OWN ADVENTURE® is a registered
trademark of Bantam Books, Inc.

Original conception of Edward Packard

Skylark Books is a registered trademark of Bantam Books, Inc.
Registered in U.S. Patent and Trademark Office
and elsewhere.

ISBN 0-553-15306-4

Published simultaneously in the United States and Canada

Bantam Books are published by Bantam Books, Inc. Its trademark, consisting of the words "Bantam Books" and the por-
trayal of a rooster, is Registered in the U.S. Patent and Trademark
Office and in other countries. Marca Registrada. Bantam
Books, Inc., 666 Fifth Avenue, New York, New York 10103.

PRINTED IN THE UNITED STATES OF AMERICA

CW   0 9 8 7 6 5 4 3 2 1

THE FLYING CARPET

READ THIS FIRST!!!

Most books are about other people.

This book is about you—and your magical flying carpet.

Do not read this book from the first page through to the last page.

Instead, start at page one and read until you come to your first choice. Decide what you want to do. Then turn to the page shown and see what happens.

When you come to the end of a story, go back and try another choice. Every choice leads to a new adventure.

Have fun with your flying carpet—but beware of wizards, genies, and the evil sultan!

Your aunt has sent you a beautiful old Persian **1** carpet from one of her trips around the world. You like it so much that you've put it right in the middle of your room.

Right now, you're sitting on the carpet and reading a book of old Arabian fairy tales. One of your favorites is about a wizard and a flying carpet.

You stop reading for a moment and gaze out the window at the starry sky. Wow, you think. A flying carpet!

Just then, your mother calls from the kitchen: "Supper's ready, dear!"

"I'll be right there, Mom!" you yell back.

You want to finish reading your story. You have just come to the part where the wizard says the magic words to make the carpet fly.

Turn to page 3.

Just for fun, you repeat the magic words out loud. *"Oozak! Popka! Kanoo!"*

All of a sudden the carpet moves beneath you.

You feel yourself rising off the floor. Before you know what's happening, the carpet whisks you out the window!

"Y-e-o-o-w!" you scream as you fall down flat. "What's going on?"

The magic words *worked*! The carpet is flying!

You grab the edges of the carpet and fearfully look down. Sure enough, there's the ground skimming by beneath you. But it looks strange—all dark and misty. In fact, everything looks strange.

"Mom!" you yell. "Where are you?"

You realize that you could jump off the carpet if you wanted to. The ground looks close.

Maybe that's what you should do. If you hang on, who knows where you'll end up?

If you jump off, turn to page 12.

If you hang on, turn to page 6.

4   You reach out, grab one end of the rope, and tug. The rope seems to be tied to something. But what? All you can see at the other end is inky blackness.

As you peer through the dark below you, you see the flying carpet again. It has swooped down and come back to you!

Now you can't make up your mind. If you get back on the carpet, it might fly you out of this darkness. On the other hand, the rope is something solid to hold on to. Maybe you should climb down it and see where it leads!

If you climb the rope, turn to page 9.

If you get back on the carpet,
turn to page 21.

6   You hang on. It's funny, but you're not so scared anymore. You even try some commands.

"Go slower!" you shout. The carpet slows down.

"Go higher!" you say. The carpet zooms up.

Soon you find that you are actually enjoying yourself.

The wind ruffles your hair as you squint your eyes against the sun.

The sun? When did it become daylight?

You look down. *That's* not your neighborhood down there! Where are you?

All at once you see a city dead ahead. But it is the strangest place you ever saw. It looks a lot like the cities you were just reading about in your book!

Turn to page 17.

8   You follow the boy. He leads you into a small white house. Just then, you notice that he has a carpet under his arm. *Your* carpet!

"Where did you get this?" you ask in surprise.

"I didn't steal it, honest!" cries the boy. "It—it fell from the sky!"

"I believe you," you say with a smile.

Suddenly there's a loud banging on the door.

"The sultan's men!" the boy whispers.

"Which way to the roof?" you ask.

The boy points to a ladder.

"Let's get up there fast!" you cry as you grab the carpet.

In a few moments you are on the roof. "Quick, jump on the carpet!" you yell.

A split second later, the two men appear on the roof, waving their swords.

Turn to page 18.

You climb down the rope.

When you get near the other end, the inky blackness suddenly disappears. You find yourself in dazzling sunlight!

You hear a man's voice.

"Ah, yes, good people, you see before you an enchanted rope. Notice how it has climbed into the air as if it were alive!"

You hear people murmuring in awe.

"Yes," the voice goes on, "I learned this trick from my father, and he learned it from his father, and . . ."

Then the speaker sees you!

Turn to page 11.

"AIEEE!" he screams.
So does everyone else.
You cling to the rope.
It must look as if you've
appeared out of thin air!

Turn to page 15.

12   You leap off the carpet—into empty black space!

What you thought was the ground is just a black cloud. And you are falling in slow motion.

"Help! Mom! *Anyone!*"

Silence greets you.

Your lower lip starts to tremble, but you tell yourself to be brave. After all, you haven't really been hurt yet.

Just then, you see an amazing sight. You can't believe your eyes.

There's a rope hanging in empty space!

Turn to page 4.

14   You zoom lower and prepare to land in the village. Now all the people are pointing and yelling.

"Who are they?" they shout. "Wizards! Genies!" someone says. "They have a flying carpet!" says another.

You and Abdul are enjoying all the attention. You decide to show off a bit.

SWOOSH! You start to zip in and out of the tiny streets just above everyone's head. You skid around a sharp corner. You are laughing so hard that you don't see the tall stack of apricots right in your path!

Now you do!

"Stop!" you scream. The carpet stops dead—but you and Abdul don't!

Turn to page 24.

"A demon! A demon!" someone yells.

You notice something funny. Everyone in the crowd is dressed like the people in your book of Arabian fairy tales!

Turn to page 28.

"Wow!" you say as you get closer.

The city sparkles in the sunlight like a jewel. Everywhere you look, you see pastel-colored houses and towers and lush gardens.

"Go down," you order the carpet. It obeys instantly and swoops down in a graceful curve. Under you is a beautiful white palace surrounded by a walled garden.

You tell the carpet to land in a courtyard right outside the wall.

"I wonder where everyone is?" you say.

As if in answer, you hear a clip-clop, clip-clop. . . . Someone is coming around the bend on a horse!

Should you wait to see who it is, or should you climb over the wall to hide in the garden until you know what's going on?

If you wait for the rider, turn to page 33.

If you hide in the garden, turn to page 37.

18   *"Oozak! Popka! Kanoo!"* you shout.

ZOOM! The carpet takes off just as one of the men swings his sword. HISSS! He cuts off a corner of the carpet. But strangely enough, the piece keeps flying alongside you! In a few moments you are all safely in the air.

You smile with relief as you turn to the boy. "What's your name?" you ask.

"Abdul," says the boy.

You are about to say more when you notice that you are flying over a desert. Maybe you should stop and figure out what to do next. But you're not even sure the carpet will obey your commands.

On the other hand, it might be a good idea to get as far away from the sultan's men as possible.

If you stop in the desert, turn to page 22.

If you keep on flying, turn to page 27.

You get back onto the carpet. All of a sudden the blackness disappears. You find yourself flying over the rooftops of your own neighborhood.

"I want to go home!" you say, as if the carpet could understand you. Then the carpet swoops down, and you *see* your own house directly ahead. Maybe the carpet *does* understand!

The carpet flies right up to your window and stops. Without wasting a second, you scramble back into your room. As soon as you're safely inside, the carpet flies off into the night. You watch until it disappears.

Just then your mother comes in. "I told you supper was ready, dear," she says. Then she looks at the floor. "Why, where's the nice carpet that your aunt gave you?" she asks.

You look out the window.

"If I told you, Mom," you answer, "you wouldn't believe me!"

The End

22   "Land, carpet!" you yell.

To your relief, the carpet obeys. It swoops down and lands next to a grove of date-palm trees.

While you and Abdul cool off in the shade, he tells you his story.

"I have been a beggar as long as I can remember," he says, "but I dream of being a magician. If I could do magic tricks, people would pay to see them."

You feel sorry for Abdul. While he is talking you get an idea.

"Here," you say, handing him the cut piece of carpet. "This will work as well as the carpet. You can do all sorts of tricks with it!"

Abdul beams with pleasure.

"You have made me very happy," he says. "It is all I could wish for."

You sigh. "The only thing *I* could wish for," you say, "is that this carpet would take me home!"

All of a sudden, your eyes begin to feel heavy. You can hardly keep them open. . . .

Turn to page 39.

24 SQUASH! SQUISH! You both fly right into the middle of the ripe apricots!

What an orange mess!

You and Abdul look at each other and start to giggle again.

"Oh well," you say as you lick your fingers. "We *were* hungry, Abdul. I hope you like apricot jam!"

The End

You run back to the shop and hop into one of the baskets. You put the cover back on from the inside just as the sultan's men come down the street.

"The demon ran this way!" one of them shouts.

"Yes! Quickly—we will trap it on the next street," says the other.

Phew, that was close!

You are just about to relax when you feel something long and slithery around your feet.

Something's in the basket with you!

Turn to page 51.

You keep flying. The endless desert slowly passes by beneath you. In the meantime, you're getting the hang of flying the magic carpet. It obeys your every command.

"This is fun!" shouts Abdul. You agree. You're not even afraid anymore.

In fact, you and Abdul are starting to think about other things—like food!

Finally you see a small village up ahead.

"Let's stop there," you shout. "Maybe we can get something to eat." Abdul nods in agreement.

You circle the village. Everyone is gaping up at you. You are just about to land when you remember what happened the last time you appeared out of nowhere.

Everyone thought you were a demon!

Maybe you should land somewhere outside the village and walk in.

If you try to land in the village, turn to page 14.

If you try to land outside the village, turn to page 31.

28 You jump off the rope.

"Wait a minute," you shout. "I'm no demon, I'm . . ."

But you never finish because suddenly, two huge men are coming after you—with swords!

"We will cut off the demon's head and bring it to the sultan!" they shout.

Your only chance is to run!

ZOOM! You zip around a corner and into a long winding street.

At the end of the street, you whiz by a shop with large covered baskets in front of it. A sign says: Ahmed, the Snake Charmer. You skid around another corner and run right into . . .

. . . a dead end! You're finished!

Then you remember the baskets. You could hide there! You whirl around just as you hear: "Psst! Follow me!"

It's a ragged little boy beckoning you. Should you trust him, or should you go back and hide in a basket?

If you follow the boy, turn to page 8.

If you hide in a basket, turn to page 25.

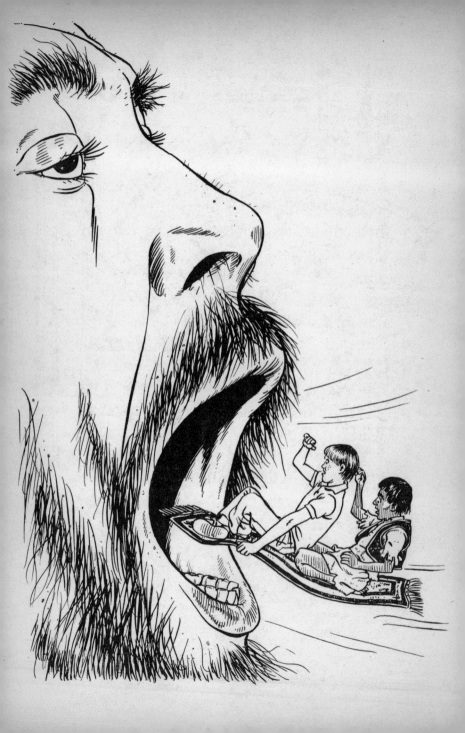

You decide to land outside the village. You head for a large hill and swoop over it in a graceful movement.

All of a sudden Abdul yells, "Look, a giant genie!"

"A giant *what*?" you ask.

"A genie—a magic being!" yells Abdul.

Then you see the genie. He's as big as a ten-story building!

He must have been taking a nap on the other side of the hill.

Now he lifts the top part of his body up and stretches his arms. His huge mouth opens in a Y-A-W-N . . . and you are being sucked into it!

"Oh, no!" you yell as you, Abdul, and the magic carpet head right for the genie's mouth.

GULP!

The End

You decide to wait for the rider. **33**

When he comes around the bend, you see that he's a man wearing a turban.

On top of that, he's riding a *mechanical horse*!

"Wow!" you whisper as you watch in awe.

The turbaned rider stops next to you.

"Ah, my young friend," he says, "I see you like my little toy."

"Little toy?" you say. "This is great!"

"My name is Perviz, and this is my humble invention," the man goes on. "I have high hopes of winning the sultan's race this morning with it."

You ask Perviz if you can come along and watch.

"You can do better than that, my young friend," he answers. "You can ride this horse in the race!"

Turn to page 38.

34   You hand the carpet to Perviz to hold.

While he takes it, he clears his throat and says, "Ahem. By the way, my young friend, I forgot to tell you one thing. The sultan has an odd habit."

"Oh? What's that?" you ask.

"He puts all the losers in jail!"

"What! Why?" you ask in surprise.

"It makes for a better race," Perviz answers with a shrug. "No one wants to lose!"

You are just about to say more when the sultan shouts: "Let the race begin!"

Before you know what's happening, the mechanical horse takes off like a shot. But it has only gone a few paces when—SPROONG! BOOINNG!

The horse has popped a spring! It slows down to a clanking walk.

You have hardly begun and you've already lost! On top of that, a big, mean-looking guard is running up to you. You haven't got a chance of escaping!

The End

You hop over the garden wall. **37**

"Aha, thief! Caught you!" a gruff voice says as a hand grabs your arm. You turn around in fright. A tall man in a black robe is glaring at you. You recognize his clothing from your book. He's a wizard!

"I saw you fly down here on my carpet!" shouts the wizard. "So *you're* the one who stole it!"

"Let me go! I didn't steal anything!" you shout, kicking and struggling.

One of your kicks hits the wizard right in the shin. "Ouch!" he yells as he releases his grip.

You scoot away with the carpet under your arm. You start to dash through the garden. Then you think it might be a good idea to run into the palace. Maybe someone there might help you.

*If you run through the garden,
turn to page 48.*

If you run into the palace, turn to page 41.

38   Perviz explains that he is too heavy to ride his mechanical horse in the race.

"With you riding him, he will be faster!"

When you arrive at the race course, you see that everyone is already there.

"The sultan himself is going to award the prize," whispers Perviz. "Twenty pieces of gold!"

You nod as you mount the mechanical horse and take your place with the other horses.

But wait! You almost forgot about your carpet. You can't hold onto it while you're racing. Maybe you should give it to Perviz to hold. But can you trust him to take care of it? Maybe you should just shove it under your saddle instead.

If you put the carpet under your saddle,
turn to page 43.

If you give the carpet to Perviz to hold,
turn to page 34.

You try to keep your eyes open, but you can't. It feels as if the carpet is moving, but you're not sure. You feel so sleepy. . . .

Suddenly your eyes snap open. You're wide awake again. You look around.

You're back in your room! Did the carpet grant your wish, or was it all a dream?

You look down. There's a piece missing from the corner of the carpet!

"Wow!" you yell.

Just then your mother comes into the room.

"I've been calling you for the last half hour!" she says. "What *is* the matter with you?"

"Uh—nothing, Mom," you say. "I was just enjoying my book."

"Well, take your head out of the clouds and come to supper," she says.

You smile as you leave your room. Your mom will never know how close to the truth she came!

The End

You run into the palace—
and bump right into a beautiful
girl!

"Where are you running to?"
asks the girl with a little smile.
You tell her that a wizard is
after you.

Go on to the next page.

42   "In that case," she says, "come to my quarters. You will be safe there."

On the way, the girl tells you her name is Sarina.

"I am a prisoner in this palace," she tells you. "The prince who lives here kidnapped me because he heard I was a wonderful cook. He has ordered me to make him the most delicious dish he has ever eaten.

"But so far he is bored with everything I make," Sarina continues. "And he won't let me go until I please him."

Turn to page 47.

You shove the carpet under your saddle and **43** line up with the other racers. "Go!" the sultan shouts, and the race begins. You're off!

But all of a sudden—SPROONG! BOOINNG!

Your mechanical horse has popped a spring! The horse slows down to a clanking walk. You haven't got a chance of winning!

Wait a minute! You have an idea.

"*Oozak! Popka! Kanoo!*" you whisper to your carpet. "Fly low."

Go on to the next page.

44   As soon as you give the command, your horse's hooves lift a few inches off the ground. The carpet is lifting you both! You glide through the air past all the other horses. Then you breeze over the finish line to win!

Then you get·an idea.

"Let's go to the kitchen," you say. "Maybe I can help you. I know a dish that *everyone* loves!"

"Really?" says Sarina.

"Trust me," you answer with a smile. "Now let's get started. . . ."

An hour later, you and Sarina are standing before the prince.

"What have you brought me this time?" He scowls. "It looks strange."

Sarina begs him to take a bite. "My friend says you will love it."

"Hmmmph," the prince sniffs, but he takes a bite anyway.

"Mmmmm," he says with his mouth full, "delicious! I *do* love it! Teach my cook to make this and you can go free."

Sarina looks at you and smiles happily.

"What do you call this marvelous dish?" she whispers.

"Spaghetti and meatballs!" you say with a grin.

The End

48 You run through the garden as fast as you can. You scurry through a grove of bushes and come out the other side. You are sure that you've escaped when suddenly you see the wizard in front of you.

How did he get there?

"So, my little carpet thief," he snarls. "Trying to get away, are you? That *proves* you're guilty!"

"No, wait!" you yell, but the wizard is already pointing a finger at you.

POOF! Something is happening—you're shrinking!

In the wink of an eye, you find yourself as small as a mouse and trapped inside a bottle!

Not only that, but you're also in the middle of a lonely desert.

"That's what I do to carpet thieves!" you hear the wizard's voice saying a long way off.

You groan and sit down in the bottle. Your only hope is that someone will pass by and let you out. But from the looks of the place, that could be a long, long time from now.

The End

You have a funny feeling you know what's in the basket, too.

You peek down at your feet. You were right—it's a snake!

And not just any snake, either. You have had the bad luck to come face to face with one of the most deadly snakes in the world—a king cobra! You're finished!

The End

52   The sultan comes over and hands you a bag of gold. "By my beard," he says, "that was a wonderful feat!"

Perviz comes running over too. "We shall share the prize money, my young friend," he says, beaming. "How did you do it?"

"Er—I think I'll keep that little secret under my hat—er, I mean my saddle!" you say.

The End

ABOUT THE AUTHOR

Jim Razzi is the bestselling author of numerous game, puzzle, and story books, including the Sherluck Bones Mystery-Detective series, and *The Genie in the Bottle* and *Dragons!* in the Bantam Skylark Choose Your Own Adventure series. Well over two and a half million copies of his books have been sold in the United States, Great Britain, and Canada. One, *The Star Trek Puzzle Manual,* was on the *New York Times* bestseller list for a number of weeks. His book *Don't Open This Box!* was picked as one of the "Books of the Year" by the Child Study Association.

ABOUT THE ILLUSTRATOR

Frank Bolle studied at Pratt Institute. He has worked as an illustrator for many national magazines and now creates and draws cartoons for magazines as well. He has also worked in advertising and children's educational materials and has drawn and collaborated on several newspaper comic strips, including *Annie.* A native of Brooklyn Heights, New York, Mr. Bolle now works and lives in Westport, Connecticut.

CHOOSE YOUR OWN ADVENTURE®

GROWING UP IS FUN WHEN YOU CHOOSE YOUR OWN ADVENTURE!

There are Choose Your Own Adventure® books for readers of all ages . . .

Your First Adventure—stories to be read aloud to preschoolers ages three to six.

Choose Your Own Adventure books in easy-to-read Skylark size for readers ages seven to nine.

Pocket-sized **Choose Your Own Adventure** books for readers ages nine and up.

And introducing **Walt Disney Choose Your Own Adventure,** storybooks for beginning readers, featuring everyone's favorite Disney characters—Snow White, Pinocchio, Dumbo, Cinderella, and more. Every page in full color!

Now you can have your favorite Choose Your Own Adventure® Series in a variety of sizes. Along with the popular pocket size, Bantam has introduced the Choose Your Own Adventure® series in a Skylark edition and also in Hardcover.

Now not only do you get to decide on how you want your adventures to end, you also get to decide on what size you'd like to collect them in.

SKYLARK EDITIONS

☐	15238	The Circus #1 E. Packard	$1.95
☐	15207	The Haunted House #2 R. A. Montgomery	$1.95
☐	15208	Sunken Treasure #3 E. Packard	$1.95
☐	15233	Your Very Own Robot #4 R. A. Montgomery	$1.95
☐	15308	Gorga, The Space Monster #5 E. Packard	$1.95
☐	15309	The Green Slime #6 S. Saunders	$1.95
☐	15195	Help! You're Shrinking #5 E. Packard	$1.95
☐	15201	Indian Trail #8 R. A. Montgomery	$1.95
☐	15190	Dream Trips #9 E. Packard	$1.95
☐	15191	The Genie In the Bottle #10 J. Razzi	$1.95
☐	15222	The Big Foot Mystery #11 L. Sonberg	$1.95
☐	15223	The Creature From Millers Pond #12 S. Saunders	$1.95
☐	15226	Jungle Safari #13 E. Packard	$1.95
☐	15227	The Search For Champ #14 S. Gilligan	$1.95
☐	15241	Three Wishes #15 S. Gilligan	$1.95
☐	15242	Dragons! #16 J. Razzi	$1.95
☐	15261	Wild Horse Country #17 L. Sonberg	$1.95
☐	15262	Summer Camp #18 J. Gitenstein	$1.95
☐	15270	The Tower of London #19 S. Saunders	$1.95
☐	15271	Trouble In Space #20 J. Woodcock	$1.95
☐	15283	Mona Is Missing #21 S. Gilligan	$1.95
☐	15303	The Evil Wizard #22 A. Packard	$1.95

Prices and availability subject to change without notice.

Buy them at your local bookstore or use this handy coupon for ordering:

Bantam Books, Inc., Dept. AVSK, 414 East Golf Road, Des Plaines, Ill. 60016

Please send me the books I have checked above. I am enclosing $_____ (please add $1.25 to cover postage and handling). Send check or money order—no cash or C.O.D.'s please.

Mr/Ms _____

Address _____

City/State _____ Zip _____

AVSK—2/85
Please allow four to six weeks for delivery. This offer expires 8/85.